will

This book belongs to:

Warrior _____

will

God's Mighty Warrior

By Sheila Walsh
Illustrated by Meredith Johnson

A Division of Thomas Nelson Publishers
Since 1798

www.thomasnelson.com

Text © 2006 by Sheila Walsh

Illustrations © 2006 by Tommy Nelson®, a Division of Thomas Nelson, Inc.

All rights reserved. No portion of this book may be reproduced in any form without the written permission of the publisher, with the exception of brief excerpts in reviews.

Published in Nashville, Tennessee, by Tommy Nelson®, a Division of Thomas Nelson, Inc.

Scripture quoted from the *International Children's Bible*®, *New Century Version*®, copyright © 1986, 1988, 1999 by Tommy Nelson®, a Division of Thomas Nelson, Inc., Nashville, Tennessee 37214.

Tommy Nelson® books may be purchased in bulk for educational, business, fundraising, or sales promotional use. For information, please e-mail SpecialMarkets@ThomasNelson.com.

Library of Congress Cataloging-in-Publication Data

Walsh, Sheila, 1956–

  Will, God's mighty warrior / by Sheila Walsh ; illustrated by Meredith Johnson.

    p. cm.

  Summary: Will, who loves to play at being a warrior, is excited when his father tells him about God's armor and that there are real enemies to be fought, both in the world and in his own heart.

  ISBN 1-4003-0805-4 (hardcover)

  [1. Christian life—Fiction. 2. Imagination—Fiction. 3. Play—Fiction. 4. Family life—Fiction.]   I. Johnson, Meredith, ill. II. Title.

PZ7.W16894Wil 2005

[E]—dc22

2005037686

Printed in China

06 07 08 09 10 RRD 5 4

This book
is dedicated to all
God's mighty warriors.
Even if you feel small,
you're mighty in
God's eyes!

Will was a warrior. He loved adventure more than bubble gum (even though he *did* hold the title for the biggest bubble blown with only nine pieces of gum).

Will was a superhero . . . sort of. He could leap over tall buildings in a single bound.

He could rescue a small child from the mouth of a ferocious beast.

He could hold his breath under water for what *had* to be hours.

Each morning, Will had a very detailed routine:

1. He would check on his baby sister, Lola.
2. He would feed his dog, Ralph the Great.
3. He would recite his pledge: "I am Will, righter of wrongs, defender of the weak, and squisher of all things evil. I raise my legendary sword and shield this day and will do battle as Will, the Mighty Warrior!"

Will's mother insisted on breakfast before battle. The breakfast table became its own battleground.

"Mom, have you ever heard of a mighty warrior eating bananas and oatmeal?" Will asked one morning.

"No," she agreed. "But have you ever heard of a mighty warrior with no muscles?"

Will flexed his muscles as if to put that worry to rest.

Will and his best friend, Josh, met in the fort after breakfast.

"Our mission today," Will announced, "is to rid the forest of all wild beasts so that Princess Lola will be able to stroll safely beneath the trees."

"It's really more of a crawl with Lola," Josh pointed out.

"Well, yes, but it should be a safe crawl," Will added.

"Agreed," Josh said.

They began the perilous journey through the forest.

"Look out!" Josh cried.

"Did you see that?" Will asked. "It was a humongous snake!"

"I know! I saw it with my own eyes," Josh confirmed.

Deeper and deeper into the forest they went.

"Keep alert at all times," Will said. "Our very lives depend on it."

"Our very lives," Josh echoed.

Suddenly there was a movement in the bushes just ahead.
They drew their swords.

Josh was about to defend himself against the monstrous
beast when Will stopped him.

"Fear not, friend," he said. "I have tamed this wild creature and now use it to serve me. Fetch us some refreshment, beast!"

Ralph the Great trotted off to look for a bone.

That night Will lay tucked in bed as his dad read to him. He was almost asleep when he heard something that made him stand straight up in the bed.

"Read that bit again, Dad," he asked.

"'Wear God's armor so that you can fight against the devil's evil tricks.'"

"Whooa!" Will's eyes grew wide. "What kind of armor does God have?"

"God's armor is what all of God's children wear for protection," Dad replied.

"Is there a sword?" Will asked.

"Absolutely!" his dad said.

"What about a shield?"

"It says here that there is a shield that can stop burning arrows," he told Will, whose eyes were now the size of saucers. "Now go to sleep, my little warrior. Tomorrow is another day."

The next morning Will was full of questions. "Dad, where do you get God's armor?"

"You ask God for it every day."

"But where does He keep it?" Will asked. "Does He have a fort like Josh and me?"

"God doesn't need a fort," Dad replied. "The whole world is God's fort."

"So what do we need the armor for?" Will continued.

"We need the armor to fight off the bad guys," Dad replied.

"Bad guys!" Will answered excitedly. "I just *knew* there would be bad guys! How cool is that!"

"This enemy is not so cool, Will," his dad warned. "The enemy doesn't like us because we belong to God."

"Don't worry, Dad. I'll get him. I'll get him good!" Will assured. "I'm not called *Will, the Mighty Warrior* for nothing!"

His father tried to remain serious. "In the end *God* will get him, Will, but we'll need the armor to protect us."

Later Will and Josh gathered in the fort. "Okay, here's today's mission," Will began. "We must find our real swords and shields that God gives to His mighty warriors."

"Where do you think they'll be?" Josh asked.

"Well . . . God knows where our fort is, so I think they'll be buried somewhere near here," Will replied.

"Excellent strategy!" Josh said.

All morning Will and Josh crawled through the bushes.
They found an old sneaker, two bones, and a feather.

"Oooh, look . . . a broken end from the enemy's burning arrow,"
Will said, eying the feather.

"Almost certainly," Josh agreed.

The search continued after lunch and through the afternoon until Will's mom called him inside.

"But, *Mo-om* . . . do you realize the importance of this mission?"

"The mission will have to continue tomorrow, honey," Mom replied. "Besides, you can't very well find armor in the dark, can you?"

Will muttered something about night vision, said goodbye to Josh, and reluctantly went inside.

"I couldn't find my armor, Dad," Will announced at bedtime.

"Where did you look?" his dad asked.

"Josh and I dug around by the fort, but it wasn't there," answered Will. "I guess God forgot to give us any armor."

"God would never forget you, and He offers His armor to everyone, little warrior," Dad replied. "But it isn't armor that you're able to see with human eyes."

Will was confused. "So it's invisible?" he asked, stifling a big yawn.

"We'll talk more tomorrow. Now go to sleep."

When Will awoke that morning, he immediately set out to learn more about the armor. At breakfast, he asked his dad, "So how does God's armor work if I can't even see it?"

"The battles you fight with God's armor can be in your heart, Will."

"You mean like when Papa's heart burns?" Will asked.

"No, not like that," Dad replied with a grin. "Do you ever get angry and want to say something mean to someone else or hurt their feelings?"

"Sometimes." Will thought for a moment. "Especially if it's that girl Gigi wanting me to dress up in some dumb prince costume!"

"Right, and do you ever want to tell a lie because you think you won't get caught?" his dad continued.

"Nooo, never!" Will said. "Oops, I think I just did. . . ."

"That's what I mean, Will," Dad explained. "Those are the battles that you can't see with your eyes, but they are real—just like God's armor."

"So it *is* invisible?" Will questioned, looking down for a trace of the armor.

"Yes, Will, but it is very powerful."

Later that day, Will and Josh went to the fort. "I think being God's warrior is a bit more complicated than I thought," Will said.

"What do you mean?" Josh asked.

"Well, we're going to need two sets of armor," Will explained. "We need one set for battles in the wild, untamable forest. And we need another set for the battles in our hearts—like the battle *not* to tell the teacher that Ralph ate our homework."

"Wow. That *is* tough," Josh agreed.

"I guess I'll have to change my pledge a little," Will said, raising his trusty sword to the sky.

"I am Will, righter of wrongs, defender of the weak, and squisher of all things evil. I raise my legendary sword and shield this day and will do battle as Will, God's Mighty Warrior!"

Finally, be strong in the Lord and in his great power. Wear the full armor of God. Wear God's armor so that you can fight against the devil's evil tricks.

Ephesians 6:10-11